SPOTTER'S GUIDE TO
FLAGS
OF THE WORLD

William Crampton

Flag images by EPSflags.com

Edited by Tori Large and Lisa Watts
Designed by Adam Constantine
Series designer: Laura Fearn
Consultant: Jos Poels

Picture acknowledgements: p.1 © Bruce Adams, Eye Ubiquitous/Corbis;
p.2-3 © Galen Rowell/Corbis; p.4-5 © Getty Images/M. Llorden; p.6-7
background © Digital Vision; p.10-11 © Charles & Josette Lenars/Corbis;
p.56-57 © Joseph Sohm, ChromoSohm In./Corbis;
maps © Craig Asquith/European Map Graphics Ltd.

First published in 2002 by Usborne Publishing Ltd., First published in
America in 2003. UE. Usborne House, 83-85 Saffron Hill, London, EC1N
8RT, England. www.usborne.com

Copyright © 2002, 1980 Usborne Publishing Ltd.
The name Usborne and the devices ♀☂ are Trade Marks of Usborne
Publishing Ltd.

Printed in Spain

The flags of twelve countries
surround the South Pole, which
is marked by the ceremonial
pole, a shiny sphere on a post

CONTENTS

HOW TO USE THIS BOOK

This book is a guide to the national flags of nearly 200 countries. The flags of all the countries in each continent, or region, of the world are grouped together. The continents appear in the contents list on page 3.

When you spot a flag, make a note of its shape, pattern and design, and emblem if it has one. If it looks like any of the flags on pages 8-9, you can then go to the pages listed and find the picture exactly like your flag.

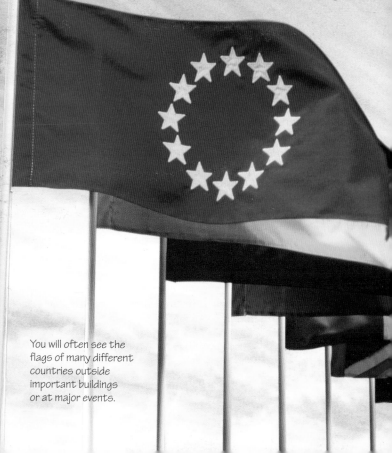

You will often see the flags of many different countries outside important buildings or at major events.

If the flag does not appear on page 8 or 9, simply flip through the rest of the book to find a picture that looks like the flag you have seen.

CHANGING FLAGS

The flags of the world are often changing. New flags are invented as new countries are created or their situation changes. You will need to look out for information on new or changing flags.

For details of websites that will help you to do this, go to the Usborne Quicklinks Website at **www.usborne-quicklinks.com** and enter the keywords "spotters flags". Before using the Internet, please read the Internet safety guidelines on the Usborne Quicklinks Website.

FLAG SPOTTING

Look for flags flying on government buildings and the embassies of foreign countries. You may also see them outside hotels, campsites and exhibition halls. Flags that appear on television count too. Watching the world news is a great way to spot flags.

When you identify a flag, mark the circle next to its picture. On pages 58-61 there is a chart where you can keep a record of all the flags you see and when you see them.

If you spot any flags which do not appear in this book, there is a blank space for their names at the end of the chart.

Flag	Date spotted
Barbados	8/6
Belize	8/6
Canada	5/7
Costa Rica	10/11
Cuba	10/11

Fill in the chart like this.

FLAG DESIGN

Many different elements make up a flag's design, and each flag is different. However, there are some popular types of basic flag design which are used by several countries. Examples of these are shown below.

Vertical stripes – this type of flag is called a "tricolore"

Horizontal stripes – with two or three stripes

Stripes with an emblem – these are easy to recognize

Stripes with a triangle – the least common of the designs

If you look at these flags, you can see what makes each design different from the rest. Some flags are bright and bold, while others are more plain or dark. Some flags have pictures or emblems on them, others are striped or have stars.

Many countries use shades of blue to represent rivers, oceans or the sky, and green to represent land, trees or the religion Islam.

SHAPE

The shape of a flag is part of its design. Most flags are rectangular, but other shapes are used too. A flag's length compared to its width gives you its proportions.

Length

On the pages of this book every flag is shown in its correct proportions, even though they are much smaller than in real life.

EMBLEMS

Some countries invent a special symbol to go on their flag. An example of this is the famous maple leaf that appears on Canada's flag.

Other countries put their national coat of arms on their flag. This may appear on the flag all the time or, in some countries, only on the government flag. The coat of arms pictured appears on the flag of Slovakia.

CLUES TO FLAGS

Some countries use similar designs in their flags to show that they are friendly with one another, or share the same religion. The following section shows some of the most popular flag designs and will help you to find them in this book.

RED, YELLOW AND GREEN FLAGS

Many West African countries use red, yellow and green in their flags, often with a star emblem as well. You can find flags like these in the Africa section of this book, on pages 38-47. The exceptions to this are Guyana and Bolivia (South America) and Grenada in the Caribbean (Central America), which also use red, yellow and green.

Guinea

Ghana

Jordan

Kuwait

RED, WHITE, BLACK AND GREEN

A flag using red, white, black and green in its design probably belongs to an Arab country. They can be found in the Asia section on pages 30-37. One exception to this is Kenya, in East Africa.

RED, WHITE AND BLACK

Red, white and black is another combination used by Arab countries, often seen with a green star as well. You will find these flags in the Asia section of this book on pages 30-37.

Iraq

Yemen

8

FLAGS WITH CROSSES

A cross with arms of uneven length, like the ones on the right, is called a "Scandinavian cross". Any flag with a cross like this belongs to a Scandinavian country and will be found in the Europe section on pages 20-29.

Iceland

Denmark

STARS AND CRESCENTS

The stars and crescent moon shape are symbols of the religion Islam. A flag with these symbols on it almost certainly belongs to a country with Islam as its main religion. Most of these flags are found in the Asia section on pages 30-37.

Turkey

Algeria

SOUTHERN CROSS

This is the name given to a pattern of stars seen in the night sky in the southern part of the world. This pattern is used in the flags of some countries in Australasia, on pages 48-51.

Samoa

New Zealand

FLAGS WITH A UNION JACK

Some countries which are, or used to be, part of the British Empire have a small Union Jack in the corner. These flags appear in the Australasia section of the book on pages 48-51.

Australia

Fiji

FLAGS IN HISTORY

Flags were originally used to identify armies and important people, such as kings or queens.

THE FIRST FLAGS

Flags were first seen 5,000 years ago in China, when bright silk flags were used in battle and religious processions.

THE ROMANS

2,000 years ago, the Romans used a kind of flag called a "standard". These flags, carried by standard-bearers, were used to identify armies.

THE CRUSADES

During the Crusades, knights carried flags with their own personal emblem. King Richard the Lionheart of England (1189-99) used the symbol of three lions and wore it on his clothing.

Richard the Lionheart's shield

This symbol is still used today on the British Royal Standard, the official flag of the queen or king.

Roman "standards" looked very different from our modern flags.

PIRATE FLAGS

In the 17th century, pirates used flags to terrify other ships at sea. Their flags, known as "Jolly Rogers", usually had a picture of a skull and crossbones, or sometimes crossed swords. Today, the skull and crossbones is used to signal danger.

A "Jolly Roger"

FLAGS OF AMERICA

When American colonists first rose against their British rulers in 1775, they used a British Red Ensign (a naval flag), with white stripes added across it to represent the thirteen colonies of America.

The first United States flag

When America became independent from Britain in 1776, the Union Jack in the corner was replaced by a blue rectangle containing thirteen stars. The stars represented the thirteen original states of America. This flag was the first Stars and Stripes.

The Stars and Stripes of 1776

THE FRENCH FLAG

Blue, white and red were adopted by French revolutionaries at the time of the French Revolution (1789-1792). They wore rosettes in these shades, called "cockades".

A French "cockade"

The modern French flag, called the "tricolore", is also blue, white and red.

11

NORTH & CENTRAL AMERICA

You can match the numbers on this map of North and Central America to the flags to see where each country is situated.

← ANTIGUA AND BARBUDA

The sun on this flag represents the dawning of a new era for the people of Antigua-Barbuda. The red stands for their energy.

→ BAHAMAS

This flag represents the blue seas and golden sands of the Bahamas. The black triangle symbolizes the pride of the people.

← BARBADOS
The emblem on this flag is a broken trident. It represents independence for the people of Barbados.

→ BELIZE
The motto on this flag, *Sub umbra floreo* (I flourish in the shadow), refers to the country's time under British rule.

← CANADA
In the middle of this flag is a red maple leaf. This is the national emblem of Canada.

→ COSTA RICA
This is the only Central American flag with a red stripe.

← CUBA
This is called the "Lone Star Flag". The red, white and blue are copied from the flag of the U.S.A.

13

NORTH & CENTRAL AMERICA

➡ DOMINICA
This flag is easy to recognize. In the middle is a parrot surrounded by ten green stars.

8

9

⬅ DOMINICAN REPUBLIC
The motto above the national coat of arms reads *Dios, Patria, Libertad* (God, Fatherland, Liberty).

➡ EL SALVADOR
El Salvador's flag stands for God, Union and Liberty.

10

11

⬅ GRENADA
The design on this flag is like an envelope. On the left is a nutmeg, which is the island's main product.

➡ GUATEMALA
This flag has a scroll on it. It shows the date when Guatemala first became independedent from Spanish rule: 15 September 1821.

12

14

← HAITI
The first Haitian flag
was created by ripping
apart a French flag and
removing the white stripe.

13

→ HONDURAS
The five blue stars in
the middle of this flag
represent the five countries
of Central America.

14

← JAMAICA
This is the only national
flag with a diagonal
cross and this combination
of yellow, green and black.

15

→ MEXICO
This is similar to Italy's
flag. The emblem shows
an eagle, snake and cactus,
from a story about the
founding of the nation's
capital, Mexico City.

16

← NICARAGUA
This is very like El
Salvador's flag, but the
blue is a slightly different
shade. The emblem shows
the national coat of arms.

17

NORTH & CENTRAL AMERICA

➡ PANAMA

This flag is often seen on ships. It is based on the flag of the U.S.A.

18

19

⬅ ST. KITTS & NEVIS

The two stars on this flag represent hope and liberty for the people.

➡ ST. LUCIA

This flag symbolizes the island's volcanic hills, beaches, and blue seas.

20

21

⬅ ST. VINCENT AND THE GRENADINES

The three diamonds on this flag represent the islands of St. Vincent.

➡ TRINIDAD AND TOBAGO

This is the only flag in the Commonwealth to use a design like this.

22

23

⬅ U.S.A.

The Stars and Stripes has a star for each U.S. state, and stripes for the original thirteen colonies.

SOUTH AMERICA

French Guiana. This belongs to France and does not have a flag of its own.

You can match the numbers on this map of South America to the flags to see where each country is situated.

→ ARGENTINA
The sun represents the day Argentina became independent from Spain. It was sunny with blue skies.

← BOLIVIA
On this flag, red is for bravery, yellow reflects the country's wealth and green represents the land.

SOUTH AMERICA

➡ BRAZIL
This emblem shows the
night sky over Brazil
and the national motto
in Portuguese: *Order
and Progress.*

3

4

⬅ CHILE
The Chilean flag is
based on the Stars and
Stripes design. It was issued
in 1817, when Chile became
independent from Spain.

➡ COLOMBIA
The yellow stripe on
this flag is as wide as
the red and blue
stripes together.

5

6

⬅ ECUADOR
The national coat of
arms on this flag shows
Mount Chimborazo, the
highest mountain in this
region.

➡ GUYANA
This flag is called the
Golden Arrow because
of the arrowhead design.
Green and red represent the
natural resources of Guyana.

7

➜ PARAGUAY
This flag has the
national coat of arms
on the front, and the
national seal on the back.

8

➜ PERU
Like the Canadian flag
but with no emblem.
The government flag has
the national coat of arms
in the middle.

9

➜ SURINAM
This flag was first used
in 1975, when Surinam
became independent
from the Netherlands.

10

➜ URUGUAY
This flag uses a similar
"smiling sun" emblem as
Argentina. The design is
like the flag of the U.S.A.

11

➜ VENEZUELA
The three stripes on this
flag are all of equal
width. The seven stars
represent the original seven
provinces of Venezuela.

12

19

EUROPE

You can match the numbers on this map of Europe to the flags to see where each country is situated.

◀ ALBANIA

The double-headed eagle on this flag dates back to the 15th century. Albania means "land of the eagle".

1

➡ ANDORRA

Several different versions of the shield may be used on this flag. It is rarely seen outside Andorra.

2

← ARMENIA
The red of this flag is to remember the deaths of the country's soldiers, both past and present.

3

→ AUSTRIA
A simple flag of red and white stripes. The government flag has the national arms, a black eagle, in the middle.

4

← AZERBAIJAN
This flag has three stripes: the traditional Turkish blue, green for the Islamic religion, and red for progress.

5

→ BELARUS
The Belarus flag is based on the flag used when Belarus was part of the Soviet Union.

6

← BELGIUM
The Belgian flag is almost square. At sea, a rectangular flag of the same design is flown.

7

EUROPE

← BOSNIA AND HERZEGOVINA
These stars show that Europe is safeguarding the country's independence.

→ BULGARIA
The white, green and red of this flag were first used by a group of Bulgarian revolutionaries.

← CROATIA
A red, white and blue striped flag, showing the national coat of arms.

→ CYPRUS
This flag has the shape of the island and two olive branches on it.

← CZECH REPUBLIC
This flag is similar to the flag of Poland, but with a blue triangle at the side.

→ DENMARK
Very like the flag of Switzerland, but a more rectangular shape with unequal arms.

➡ ESTONIA
On this flag, blue is for loyalty, black for past suffering and white for virtue.

14

⬅ FINLAND
Finland's flag is a blue cross on a white background. The national arms sometimes appear too.
15

➡ FRANCE
The famous tricolore design has been used by many countries.

16

17

⬅ GEORGIA
On this flag, black is Georgia's dark past and white is its bright future.

➡ GERMANY
This black, red and yellow flag has been used at various times in German history.

18

EUROPE

➡ GREECE
Like Uruguay's flag,
but the "smiling sun" is
replaced by a white cross.

19

20

⬅ HUNGARY
This flag is similar to the
flag of Iran, but the
other way up. It is also
slightly shorter.

➡ ICELAND
This flag was originally
blue and white. The red
cross was added to show a
connection with Denmark

21

22

⬅ IRELAND
The Irish flag was
designed to symbolize
unity between the people.

➡ ITALY
Italy replaced the blue
of the French Tricolore
with green for their flag.

23

24

⬅ LATVIA
This flag is very dark
red, divided in two by
a white stripe.

➡ LIECHTENSTEIN
This flag, with a crown in the top left-hand corner, is rarely seen outside Liechtenstein.

25

26

⬅ LITHUANIA
This flag was not flown from 1940 until 1989, two years before Lithuania broke away from the Soviet Union.

➡ LUXEMBOURG
This flag is longer and lighter blue than the Netherlands flag.

27

28

⬅ MACEDONIA
This flag has a red background with a golden sun in the middle.

➡ MALTA
The George Cross medal appears in the corner of this flag, so it is easy to recognize.

29

30

⬅ MOLDOVA
This design is very similar to Romania's flag and is intended to represent their history.

EUROPE

➡ MONACO
This is like the flag of Indonesia but with a slightly different shape.

31

32

➡ NORWAY
This is like Denmark's flag, but with a blue cross on top of the white.

34

⬅ NETHERLANDS
The first Dutch flag had an orange stripe, but it was changed to red.

33

➡ PORTUGAL
Behind the national coat of arms on this flag is a picture of a ship's navigating instrument.

36

⬅ POLAND
Poland's flag dates back to Medieval times.

35

⬅ ROMANIA
This flag was created in 1848 by combining two flags of the Ottoman Empire.

26

◆ **RUSSIA**
This flag replaced the red communist flag in 1991. Red, white and blue once represented Moscow.

37

38

➡ **SAN MARINO**
This blue and white flag is rarely seen outside San Marino.

39

◆ **SERBIA AND MONTENEGRO**
This flag has recently changed from the old Yugoslavian flag.

➡ **SLOVAKIA**
A white, blue and red striped flag with the coat of arms to the left.

40

41

◆ **SLOVENIA**
The design is very much like the Slovak and Russian flags.

➡ **SPAIN**
Spain's red and yellow striped flag is sometimes shown with the national coat of arms.

42

27

EUROPE

➡ SWEDEN
The flag of Sweden has a yellow cross on a blue background.

43

44

⬅ SWITZERLAND
This is the only country with a square national flag. It has strong connections with Christianity.

➡ UKRAINE
The two stripes of blue and yellow on this flag symbolize the sky, streams, mountains and golden fields.

45

⬅ VATICAN CITY
The Vatican City in Rome, the home of the Roman Catholic religion, has its own flag.
46

← UNITED KINGDOM

The Union Jack is the national flag of England, Scotland, 47 Ireland and Wales (see below), and has a unique design.

→ ENGLAND

England's flag is called the St George Cross. It makes up part of the Union Jack flag.

48

← SCOTLAND

This is the cross of St Andrew. It also makes up part of the Union Jack.

49

→ WALES

This flag does not form part of the Union Jack. The red dragon is a traditional Welsh emblem.

50

NORTHERN IRELAND

Northern Ireland does not have its own flag. The official flag used there is the Union Jack.

ASIA

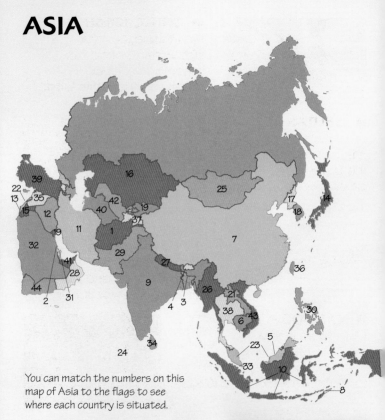

You can match the numbers on this map of Asia to the flags to see where each country is situated.

➡ **AFGHANISTAN**
The coat of arms on Afghanistan's flag has a picture of a mosque in the middle of it.

⬅ **BAHRAIN**
Like Qatar, Bahrain's flag has two sections joined in a zig-zag line.

◆ BANGLADESH
On this flag, the red disc is the sun and the green background represents the fertile land.

3

➡ BHUTAN
In the local language, Bhutan means "land of the dragon", so the flag has an emblem of a dragon.

4

5

◆ BRUNEI
The coat of arms on this flag stands for health, wealth and peace for the people of Brunei.

➡ CAMBODIA
Cambodia is one of the oldest monarchies in the world. Its flag stands for Nation, Religion and King.

6

7

◆ CHINA
Red and yellow are traditional in Chinese culture, and red also stands for communism.

➡ EAST TIMOR
This flag is like the flag of the party who fought for independence for East Timor, which was won in 2002.

8

ASIA

➡ INDIA
The blue wheel in the middle of this flag is a symbol for life and continuity.

9

10

⬅ INDONESIA
This flag is the same as the Polish flag but upside down.

➡ IRAN
This flag has a green emblem and Arabic writing on the white stripe.

11

12

⬅ IRAQ
The Arabic writing on this flag is called the *takbir*. It means God is Great.

➡ ISRAEL
The emblem on this flag is the Star of David, an important Jewish symbol.

13

14

⬅ JAPAN
In Japanese, Japan means "land of the rising sun". The red disc here represents the sun.

← JORDAN
This unusual design uses the traditional Arab red, white, green and black.

15

→ KAZAKHSTAN
The pattern along the side of this flag is the country's national emblem.

16

← KOREA, NORTH
This flag was designed in 1948. It is rarely seen outside North Korea.

17

→ KOREA, SOUTH
The circle on this flag is the "Yin-Yang", an important Chinese symbol which represents harmony.

18

← KUWAIT
This flag is the only design with this unusual cut-off triangle at the side.

19

→ KYRGYZSTAN
The symbol in the middle of this flag is the roof of a yurt (a type of tent).

20

ASIA

➡ LAOS
The white disc on this flag is the moon and the blue stripe is a river.

21

22

⬅ LEBANON
In the middle of this flag is a cedar tree. These trees grow in the mountains of Lebanon.

➡ MALAYSIA
This flag is like the Stars and Stripes. The stars are replaced by Islamic symbols.

23

24

⬅ MALDIVES
The Islamic crescent symbol on this flag shows the country's religion.

➡ MONGOLIA
The emblem on this flag is the "soyombo", a Mongolian symbol.

25

26

⬅ MYANMAR (BURMA)
Red, white and blue on this flag stand for courage, purity and peace.

34

← NEPAL
This is the only national flag of this shape. The top symbol is the moon, the lower one is the sun.

27

→ OMAN
This crossed swords and dagger design is Oman's national emblem.

28

← PAKISTAN
The white stripe on this flag stands for religions other than Muslim.

29

→ PHILIPPINES
During wartime this flag is flown upside down, with the red stripe on top.

30

← QATAR
This flag is an unusual design. It is much longer than most national flags.

31

→ SAUDI ARABIA
This Arabic writing says: "There is no God but Allah and Mohammed is the Prophet of Allah".

32

ASIA

➡ **SINGAPORE**
Red is used here to represent equality and brotherhood. White symbolizes purity.

33

34

⬅ **SRI LANKA**
Each part of this flag represents one of the religious groups in the country.

➡ **SYRIA**
A simple red, white and black Arabian flag with green stars.

35

36

⬅ **TAIWAN**
On this flag, red represents the land of China, and the sun stands for the spirit of progress.

➡ **TAJIKISTAN**
Tajikistan left the USSR in 1992. The crown and stars represent its sovereignty.

37

38

⬅ **THAILAND**
The flag of Thailand has not changed since it was first used in 1917.

← TURKEY
This red flag uses the symbols of Islam, the crescent and star.

➡ TURKMENISTAN
The pattern on this flag shows traditional carpet designs called "guls".

← UAE
The UAE (United Arab Emirates) flag uses a typical Arab design and was adopted in 1971.

➡ UZBEKISTAN
The crescent on this flag stands for the rebirth of the nation.

← VIETNAM
The five points of this star represent the farmers, workers, the youth, intellectuals and soldiers.

➡ YEMEN
This flag was issued in 1990 when North and South Yemen were united.

AFRICA

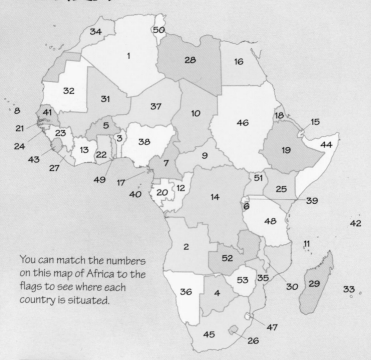

You can match the numbers on this map of Africa to the flags to see where each country is situated.

◄ ALGERIA
Another Islamic country, this flag shows the Islamic symbol of a crescent and star.

➡ ANGOLA
The emblem on this flag represents the industrial and agricultural workers of the country.

← BENIN
This flag was re-introduced in 1991, but was originally used between 1960 and 1975.

3

→ BOTSWANA
The blue on this flag is the rain needed for farming. Black and white stripes represent equality.

4

← BURKINA FASO
This red and the star symbolize the 1984 revolution. Green is for the country's natural resources.

5

→ BURUNDI
The three stars on this flag stand for "Unity, Work and Progress" – the national motto.

6

← CAMEROON
This flag uses the West African red, yellow and green. The yellow star stands for unity.

7

AFRICA

➡ **CAPE VERDE**
The ten stars on this flag represent the ten islands of Cape Verde set in a blue sea.

⬅ **CENTRAL AFRICAN REPUBLIC**
This flag shows a connection with France (red, white and blue) and Africa (red, green and yellow).

➡ **CHAD**
This flag is the same as Romania's flag. Chad was not aware of this when the design was chosen.

⬅ **COMOROS**
These four stripes and stars represent the four islands. The crescent shows its people are Islamic.

➡ **CONGO**
The flag of the Congo has red and green sections divided by a yellow stripe.

← **COTE D'IVOIRE**
The orange on this flag represents the desert, green is the woods, and white stands for unity.

13

→ **DEMOCRATIC REPUBLIC OF CONGO**
This flag has one large and six smaller yellow stars on a blue background.

14

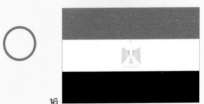

15

← **DJIBOUTI**
The blue on this flag was copied from the flag of Somalia.

→ **EGYPT**
This is the only flag of the Arab countries to have a coat of arms.

16

17

← **EQUATORIAL GUINEA**
The six stars on this coat of arms represent the mainland and five islands.

AFRICA

➡ ERITREA
A red triangle with a
yellow wreath on it
divides the green and blue
sections of this flag.

18

19

⬅ ETHIOPIA
The national coat of
arms, in the middle of
this flag, was added in 1996.

➡ GABON
Gabon's flag has
green, yellow and blue
horizontal stripes.

20

⬅ GAMBIA
This flag represents the
red sun, green land and
blue of the River Gambia.

21

➡ GHANA
The black star in the
middle of this flag
stands for liberty.

22

⬅ GUINEA
This is like the flag of
Mali but the other way
around.

23

← GUINEA-BISSAU
This West African flag has a black star like the flag of Ghana.

24

→ KENYA
This emblem shows an African warrior's shield and two crossed spears.

25

← LESOTHO
The light brown shield and spears on this flag are symbols of the national safeguards for peace.

26

→ LIBERIA
Based on the Stars and Stripes design, this flag is often seen on ships.

27

← LIBYA
Libya has been using a plain green flag since 1977. Before this it used a design similar to Egypt's flag.

28

→ MADAGASCAR
This is one of many flags using red, white and green, but the only one with this design.

29

AFRICA

➡ MALAWI
The rising sun on this flag stands for the dawning of a new era for the country.

30

31

⬅ MALI
This is a similar design to the flag of Senegal, with which Mali was once united.

➡ MAURITANIA
The main religion of Mauritania is Islam, as the flag shows.

32

33

⬅ MAURITIUS
These stripes are taken from the coat of arms of Mauritius.

➡ MOROCCO
This type of star is called Solomon's seal, and symbolizes harmony.

34

35

⬅ MOZAMBIQUE
This flag bears the national arms – a rifle and hoe crossed over an open book, on a gold star.

← NAMIBIA
The yellow sun in the corner of this flag represents life and energy.

→ NIGER
The orange disc in the middle of this flag is a symbol of the sun.

← NIGERIA
This is the only national flag with green and white vertical stripes.

→ RWANDA
This flag stands for happiness and prosperity for its people, without violence.

← SAO TOME & PRINCIPE
The two stars on this flag stand for the two islands of Sao Tome and Principe.

→ SENEGAL
The star on this flag is said to represent unity and hope.

AFRICA

➡ SEYCHELLES
The design of this flag represents a dynamic young country moving into a new future.

⬅ SIERRA LEONE
This is the only flag with green, white and blue horizontal stripes.

➡ SOMALIA
An unusual design for an African flag, Somalia copied this blue from the United Nations flag.

⬅ SOUTH AFRICA
The "pall" (Y-shape) on this flag represents the unified future of the nation.

➡ SUDAN
Another flag using the red, white, green and black combination.

⬅ SWAZILAND
This emblem shows a warrior's shield, spears and a fighting stick.

← **TANZANIA**
← TANZANIA
The diagonal stripe on this flag runs the other way to the stripe on the flag of Trinidad.

→ TOGO
The five stripes of this flag represent the five regions of the country.

← TUNISIA
This is very similar to the Turkish flag, but the crescent and star are in a white circle.

→ UGANDA
The bird in the circle in the middle of this flag is an African crane.

← ZAMBIA
An unusual design, as it has the emblem and stripes on the right.

→ ZIMBABWE
This flag shows the Zimbabwe bird, the national emblem of Zimbabwe.

AUSTRALASIA

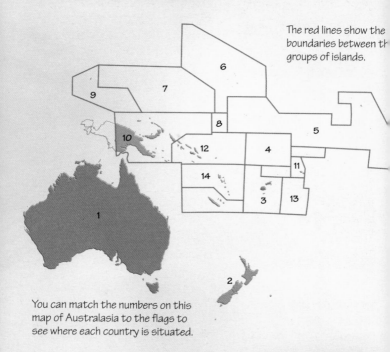

The red lines show the boundaries between th[e] groups of islands.

You can match the numbers on this map of Australasia to the flags to see where each country is situated.

➡ **AUSTRALIA**
These five small stars represent the Southern Cross, a pattern of stars seen in the night sky in the Southern part of the world.

⬅ **NEW ZEALAND**
This flag only shows four of the stars of the Southern Cross and no Commonwealth star.

← FIJI
Fiji and Tuvalu both have the Union Jack on their flag, as they belong to the British Commonwealth.

3

→ TUVALU
The nine stars on this flag represent the nine islands of Tuvalu against the turquoise oceans.

4

← KIRIBATI
The wavy lines on this flag represent the sea, with a bird flying over the sun.

5

→ MARSHALL ISLANDS
White and orange bands represent the Ratak and Ralik islands. The blue is the Pacific Ocean.

6

AUSTRALASIA

← MICRONESIA

The number of stars on this flag has changed many times, as the number of island states belonging to Micronesia has changed.

7

➡ NAURU

The white star on this flag represents the position of Nauru under the equator (the yellow stripe).

8

➡ PALAU

The disk on this flag represents the moon as a symbol of national unity and destiny.

9

← PAPUA NEW GUINEA

The Southern Cross stars on this flag indicate links with Australia. The bird is the local bird of paradise.

10

➡ SAMOA
Red and white have been used in Samoan flags throughout history. The Southern Cross stars are also used on this flag.

11

⬅ SOLOMON ISLANDS
The stars on this flag represent the five districts of the Solomon Islands.

12

➡ TONGA
This flag design was chosen for its link to Christianity. Tonga's law says that it cannot be changed.

13

⬅ VANUATU
The yellow Y-shape on this flag shows the pattern of the islands in the Pacific Ocean.

14

WORLD MAP

This world map shows where the continents are positioned in relation to each other. You can use the page numbers opposite to direct you to the flag pages for each continent.

NORTH AND CENTRAL AMERICA

EUROPE

AFRICA

SOUTH AMERICA

ASIA

AUSTRALASIA

INTERNATIONAL FLAGS

Most of the flags in this book are national flags; they belong to a single country. There are other flags, however, that represent a group of countries, an organization, or an event.

← EUROPE
The flag of Europe is blue with twelve yellow stars to represent the original twelve members of the European council.

→ BRITISH COMMONWEALTH
54 former British dependencies form the Commonwealth. The flag symbolizes its sunny future.

← UNITED NATIONS
The emblem on this flag shows a map of the world, surrounded by a wreath of olive branches, representing peace.

→ OLYMPIC GAMES
On this flag, the five rings stand for the five continents of the world. The white background stands for peace.

➡ RED CROSS

This organization is named after its flag. A red cross on a white background is the symbol of the Christian religion.

⬅ RED CRESCENT

This flag is used by the Red Cross in countries where the main religion is Islam.

➡ NATO

This is the flag of the North Atlantic Treaty Organisation. It shows the official emblem of this organization.

⬅ BUDDHISM

The horizontal stripes on this flag represent all the races of the world living in harmony. The vertical stripes stand for eternal world peace.

FLYING THE FLAG

PARTS OF A FLAG
Flags are usually made of cloth. At one side of the cloth is a tube of material called the "sleeve". This is what is used to attach the flag to the flagstaff, or pole. Here is a simple way of doing this:

Pulley

Sleeve

A short rope called the hoist rope is sewn into the sleeve

This long rope is called the halyard. The hoist rope is attached to it.

To raise the flag you pull the halyard and fasten it at the bottom of the flagstaff

Flagstaff

FLAGS AT HALF MAST
Flags are often flown at half mast after a famous person has died or during a national crisis, as a sign of respect and mourning. A flag at half mast is first raised to the top, then lowered so it is one flag's distance from the top of the pole.

FLAGS THE RIGHT WAY UP

Flying a flag upside down is a sign of surrender, so it is very important to fly it the right side up. This is easy with some flags, such as those with an emblem. With other flags, it can be more tricky.

The **Union Jack** is often flown upside down by mistake. The wide white stripe should always be above the red stripe in the top left-hand corner.

Union
Jack

Right side up   Wrong side up

FLAG FRONT AND BACK

All flags have a front, called the obverse, and a back, called the reverse. The obverse is the side you see when the pole, or flagstaff, is on the left. The reverse of the flag is usually a mirror image of the obverse.

South
African
flag

Obverse   Reverse

Some flags with an emblem are made of two pieces of cloth sewn together so that the emblem is correct on both sides.

Mexican
flag

Obverse - eagle
faces left

Reverse - eagle still
faces left

SPOTTER'S CHART

The flags listed in this chart are arranged in alphabetical order. When you see a flag, write down the date you spotted it next to the name of the flag. At the end of the chart are blank spaces for you to write down the names of any flags you see that aren't listed in this book.

Flag	Date spotted
Afghanistan	
Albania	
Algeria	
Andorra	
Angola	
Antigua and Barbuda	
Argentina	
Armenia	
Australia	
Austria	
Azerbaijan	
Bahamas	
Bahrain	
Bangladesh	
Barbados	
Belarus	
Belgium	
Belize	
Benin	
Bhutan	
Bolivia	
Bosnia & Herzegovenia	
Botswana	

Flag	Date spotted
Brazil	
Brunei	
Buddhism	
Bulgaria	
Burkina Faso	
Burma/Myanmar	
Burundi	
Canada	
Cambodia	
Cameroon	
Cape Verde	
Central African Republic	
Chad	
Chile	
China	
Colombia	
Comoros	
Congo	
Costa Rica	
Cote d'Ivoire	
Croatia	
Cuba	

Flag	Date spotted
Cyprus	
Czech Republic	
Democratic Republic of Congo	
Denmark	
Djibouti	
Dominica	
Ecuador	
Egypt	
El Salvador	
England	
Equatorial Guinea	
Eritrea	
Estonia	
Ethiopia	
Europe	
Fiji	
Finland	
France	
Gabon	
Gambia	
Georgia	
Germany	
Ghana	
Greece	
Grenada	
Guatemala	
Guinea	
Guinea-Bissau	
Guyana	
Haiti	
Honduras	

Flag	Date spotted
Hong Kong	
Hungary	
Iceland	
India	
Indonesia	
Iran	
Iraq	
Ireland	
Israel	
Italy	
Jamaica	
Japan	
Jordan	
Kazakhstan	
Kenya	
Kiribati	
Korea, North	
Korea, South	
Kuwait	
Kyrgyzstan	
Laos	
Latvia	
Lebanon	
Lesotho	
Liberia	
Libya	
Liechtenstein	
Lithuania	
Luxembourg	
Macedonia	
Madagascar	
Malawi	

Flag	Date spotted	Flag	Date spotted
Malaysia		Peru	
Maldives		Philippines	
Mali		Poland	
Malta		Portugal	
Marshall Islands		Qatar	
Mauritania		Red Crescent	
Mauritius		Red Cross	
Mexico		Romania	
Micronesia		Russia	
Moldova		Rwanda	
Monaco		Samoa	
Morocco		Sao Tome & Principe	
Mozambique		San Marino	
Myanmar/Burma		Saudi Arabia	
Namibia		Scotland	
NATO		Senegal	
Nauru		Serbia & Montenegro	
Netherlands		Seychelles	
New Zealand		Sierra Leone	
Nicaragua		Singapore	
Niger		Slovakia	
Nigeria		Slovenia	
Northern Ireland		Solomon Islands	
Norway		Somalia	
Olympic Games		South Africa	
Oman		Spain	
Pakistan		Sri Lanka	
Palau		St. Lucia	
Panama		St. Vincent	
Papua New Guinea		Sudan	
Paraguay		Surinam	

Flag	Date spotted	Flag	Date spotted
Swaziland			
Sweden			
Switzerland			
Syria			
Taiwan			
Tajikstan			
Tanzania			
Thailand			
Togo			
Tonga			
Trinidad and Tobago			
Tunisia			
Turkey			
Turkmenistan			
Tuvalu			
Uganda			
Ukraine			
United Arab Emirates			
United Kingdom			
United Nations			
Uruguay			
USA			
Uzbekistan			
Vanatua			
Vatican City			
Venezuela			
Vietnam			
Wales			
Yemen			
Zambia			
Zimbabwe			

GLOSSARY

Coat of Arms - the emblem of a country, often displayed on a cloak or shield.

Colony - a territory conquered or settled in by another nation.

Commonwealth - group of countries under the rule of one leading country, e.g. the Commonwealth of Nations.

Czar - the title of the rulers of Russia from 1547 - 1721.

Emblem - a picture or image with a specific, symbolic meaning.

Equator - an imaginary line going around the Earth, exactly between the North Pole and South Pole.

Guls - the name for a pattern used in traditional Eastern carpet making.

Liberty - freedom.

Monarchy - a government with a king or queen at its head.

Motto - a saying or phrase with a special meaning.

Province - a district within a country with its own administration.

Revolution - the overthrow of a government or social order.

Southern Cross - a formation of stars seen in the night sky in the southern part of the world

Sovereignty - the supreme authority in a country or state.

Stars and Stripes - the name given to the flag of the U.S.A.

Trident - three-pronged spear.

Union Jack - the name given to the flag of the UK.

Yurt - a type of tent in Kyrgyzstan.